HAVE YOU SEEN MIKKI OLSEN?

ALEX MACDONALD

Frances Lincoln
First Editions

The penguin loved Mikki Olsen.

Every day,

whatever the penguin did ...

Mikki Olsen was right there
next to him doing it also.

Because the last thing the penguin
wanted was to lose Mikki Olsen.

But, unfortunately,

at the end of a
very busy day ...

the penguin sat
on Mikki Olsen ...

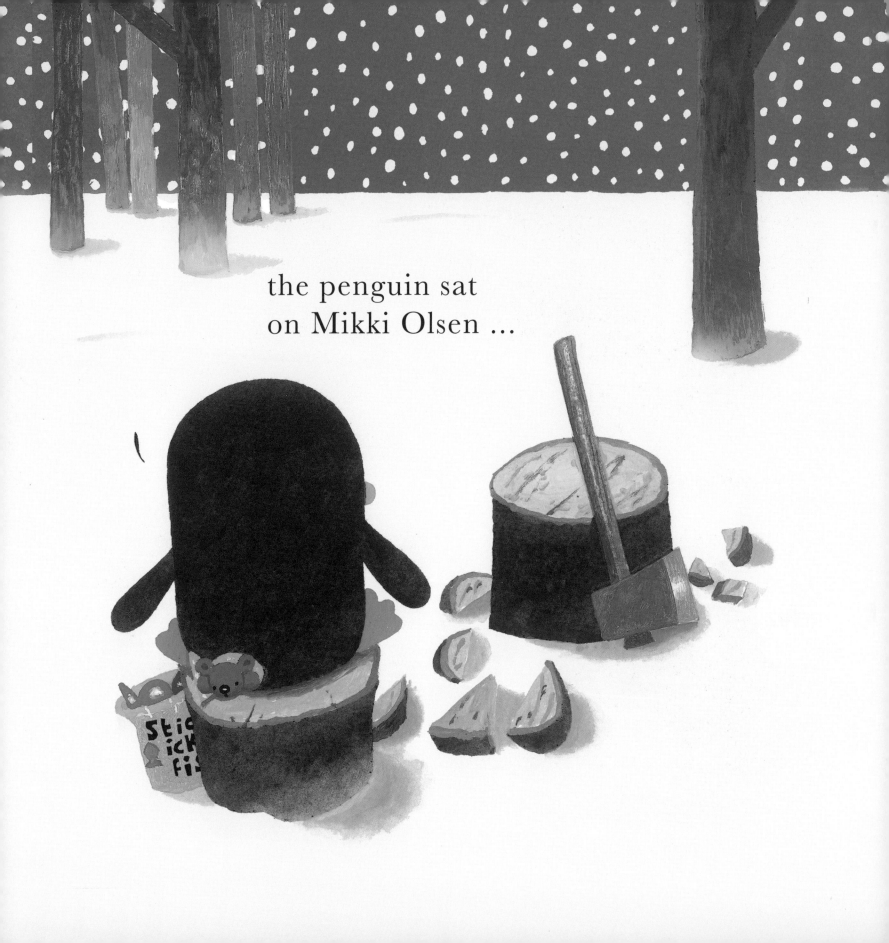

and was far too
tired to notice.

So he went home and fell asleep.

And it wasn't until the next morning that the penguin realized Mikki Olsen was missing.

And began looking for him ...

here,   there

and everywhere.

And the more the penguin looked for
Mikki Olsen, the more worried he became.

'Mikki Olsen must be *somewhere*,' he thought.

But he looked in all
the *somewheres* he
could think of.

And Mikki Olsen
wasn't in any of them.

So the penguin decided that Mikki Olsen must be
in the last place a penguin would look for anything ...

But he wasn't there, either.

'This is the worst day ever,' said the penguin. And he lay in the snow and was as sad as a penguin could be.

Until, that is ...

he got up to go home
without Mikki Olsen and
saw in the penguin-shaped
hole he'd left in the snow,
a small Mikki Olsen-shaped hole.

And realized where
Mikki Olsen had
been all along ...

and said *Hello* to Mikki Olsen.

And promised to
take better care of him in future.
Because, whatever the penguin did ...

he wanted Mikki Olsen to be
right there next to him doing it also.

For my brother

For Rowan, Archie, Nelly-Lovelle,

Poppy, and Lily Bellhouse, my first reader

With love and thanks to Paul, Yewande and Ros

Text and Illustrations © 2024 Alex Macdonald.

First published in 2024 by First Editions under Frances Lincoln Children's Books,
an imprint of The Quarto Group.
1 Triptych Place, London, SE1 9SH
T (0)20 7700 6700 F (0)20 7700 8066
www.Quarto.com

A catalogue record for this book is available from the British Library.

ISBN 978-0-7112-8530-9
eISBN 978-0-7112-8532-3
The illustrations were created with acrylic paint (and gouache solely for Mikki Olsen).
Set in Baskerville

Printed in Vilnius, Lithuania BAL102023

9 8 7 6 5 4 3 2

MIX
Paper | Supporting
responsible forestry
FSC® C107574
FSC
www.fsc.org